Back Pack Lilly

By: Maya "Jai" Pinson
Illustrator: Beatrice Sims

AuthorHouse™
1663 Liberty Drive
Bloomington, IN 47403
www.authorhouse.com
Phone: 1 (800) 839-8640

Published by AuthorHouse 10/28/2017

ISBN: 978-1-5462-1503-5 (sc)
ISBN: 978-1-5462-1502-8 (e)

Library of Congress Control Number: 2017916850

Print information available on the last page.

authorHOUSE®

"Back Pack Lilly" is dedicated to my sister Brittany and my niece Janiya, whom I look at as my little sister.

Having Janiya as my niece makes me the luckiest Aunt in the world. I love Janiya dearly; she has such a big piece of my heart.

Dad, Mom, Nana, Papa and my brother DJ – thank you for supporting me in everything I do. I love you all very much.

When we wake up in the morning,
We are excited to play.

We dress and gather our toys
to start our fun-filled day.

We bounce the ball for hours beside our playhouse called "The Shack."

Here comes Lilly running with
Alex's large back pack.

Alexis yells, "Oh no, Lilly!
What are you doing?"

We peek inside the back pack...
Our day of fun is ruined!

As we sit down on the ground
to study really hard,

Lilly runs between us and moves our playing cards!

Once we finish studying, we put the blocks in a stack.

Here comes Lilly running again
with Alexis's back pack.

Lilly wiggles and wiggles the back pack
Until the pens and papers fall out,

and Mommy yells "Do
your homework!"
We start to pout.

We sit back on the ground and think
that learning is so much fun.

As soon as we finish our work,
Alex yells, "We're done!"

We jump up and start running
back over to The Shack.

Lilly starts to chase us... this time with no back pack!

CPSIA information can be obtained
at www.ICGtesting.com
Printed in the USA
BVOW05s1859050218
507282BV00018B/229/P